This book belongs to:

_____

_____

_____

To Kiki ~ C P

To my sister Alex Macnaughton ~ T M

LITTLE TIGER PRESS

An imprint of Magi Publications

1 The Coda Centre, 189 Munster Road, London SW6 6AW

www.littletigerpress.com

First published in Great Britain 2009

This edition published 2010

Text copyright © Caroline Pitcher 2009

Illustrations copyright © Tina Macnaughton 2009

Caroline Pitcher and Tina Macnaughton have asserted their rights

to be identified as the author and illustrator of this work under the

Copyright, Designs and Patents Act, 1988

A CIP catalogue record for this book is available from the British Library

Printed in Singapore

2 4 6 8 10 9 7 5 3 1

Time for Bed, Little One

Caroline Pitcher   Tina Macnaughton

LITTLE TIGER PRESS
London

"Time for bed, little one," said Mother Fox.
"The moon is melting away and the sun is getting up.
It's time foxes were asleep."

"But I'm not sleepy!" Little Fox said. "My friends
are only just waking. Please can I have *one* more play?"

"Just one more play then, little cub."

So Little Fox scampered off into the wood, where an owl was flying softly overhead.

"Hello, Owl! Will you play with me?" asked Fox.

"I'm on my way home to bed," hooted Owl. "And you should be too-hoo!"

"But I'm not sleepy!" Little Fox cried. And he charged into a woodland glade where Fawn was waking up.

"Play with me?" asked Little Fox.

"It's breakfast time for us," said gentle Mother Deer. "Shouldn't you be going home? The sun is turning the sky to gold and foxes should be down in their dens."

"But I'm not sleepy!" Little Fox cried and he skipped away again.

As Fox raced into the sunshine, a butterfly fluttered past his nose.

He bounded after it, jumping and bouncing, all the way to the riverbank.

Someone was busy in the water.

It was Otter! He was twisting and turning in
the rippling river, rolling through the bubbles.
"Will you play with me?" called Little Fox.
But Otter squeaked, "I'm busy now. I'm
catching fish, and dragonflies too."

"Otter's allowed to stay up all day,"
thought Little Fox. "*He* doesn't have
to go to sleep and miss everything."

Just then an acorn rolled
across the grass near Fox's paw.

He looked up and there was
Squirrel, high up on a branch.

"Catch me if you can!" she cried and dashed down the tree, shaking her shimmering tail.

They raced into the woods, through the crackly bracken . . .

. . . scattering the leaves and leaping over logs.

The woods were rich with the smell of feathers and fur and peppery leaves.

But Little Fox was getting tired and began to trail behind.

"Please wait for me," he panted. "But I've got oodles of energy left," chattered Squirrel. "Maybe you should be going to bed?"

Squirrel danced along the branch, leaping from tree to tree all the way through the woods.

Then it was quiet. Little Fox was by himself.

"It's not fair," he thought. "When I get up tonight, there will be no one left awake. I'll be all alone again."

Little Fox sighed, and padded home. He was so tired he could hardly even lift his head . . .

. . . and he nearly bumped into Badger!

"Are you off to bed, Little Fox?" Badger asked.
"I'm so tired, I can't wait to be snuggled in
my sett. Will you be there when I get up? We can
play chase in the moonlight!"

"Yes, oh yes, I will!" cried Fox,
and he trotted on home.
    At last he had a friend to
play with in the night.

Back in his den, Little Fox nestled down with his mum. She nuzzled his ears and they cuddled up safe – a cosy pile of paws and tails.

"Sleep well, my little one," his mother said. "When the moon is high and the stars crackle in the dark, you'll wake up full of life again."

And Little Fox fell fast asleep.

Cosy Little Tiger reads that will settle your little one to bed.

Snuggle Up, Sleepy Ones
Claire Freedman
Illustrated by Tina Macnaughton

Don't be Afraid, Little Ones
M Christina Butler   Caroline Pedler

The Bears in the Bed and the Great Big Storm
Paul Bright   Jane Chapman

I Love You as BIG as the World
David Van Buren   Tim Warnes

Bedtime for Little Bears!
David Bedford   Caroline Pedler

Under the Silvery Moon
COLLEEN McKEOWN

For information regarding any of the above titles
or for our catalogue, please contact us:
Little Tiger Press, 1 The Coda Centre,
189 Munster Road, London SW6 6AW
Tel: 020 7385 6333 Fax: 020 7385 7333
E-mail: info@littletiger.co.uk
www.littletigerpress.com